AFTERSHOCK

AFTERSHOCK

VANESSA ACTON

MINNEAPOLIS

Darby Creek
A division of Lerner Publishing Group, Inc.
241 First Avenue North
Minneapolis, MN 55401 USA

For reading levels and more information, look up this title at
www.lernerbooks.com.

The images in this book are used with the permission of: © Nigelspiers/Dreamstime. com (earthquake highway); © iStockphoto.com/ggyykk (building); © iStockphoto. com/13UG13th (dust texture); © iStockphoto.com/Duncan Walker (grunge frame); © iStockphoto.com/Marina Mariya (swirl).

Main body text set in Janson Text LT Std 12/17.5.
Typeface provided by Adobe Systems.

Library of Congress Cataloging-in-Publication Data

Names: Acton, Vanessa, author.
Title: Aftershock / by Vanessa Acton.
Description: Minneapolis : Darby Creek, [2017] | Series: Day of disaster | Summary: "A high school student and her friends are already having a rough day—and then the earthquake hits. Working through personal issues suddenly doesn't seem like such a big deal compared to struggling to stay alive"— Provided by publisher.
Identifiers: LCCN 2016019495 (print) | LCCN 2016034210 (ebook) | ISBN 9781512427776 (lb : alk. paper) | ISBN 9781512430912 (pb : alk. paper) | ISBN 9781512427851 (eb pdf)
Subjects: | CYAC: Earthquakes—Fiction. | Survival—Fiction. | Friendship—Fiction. | California—Fiction.
Classification: LCC PZ7.1.A228 Af 2017 (print) | LCC PZ7.1.A228 (ebook) | DDC [Fic]—dc23

LC record available at https://lccn.loc.gov/2016019495

Manufactured in the United States of America
1-41502-23363-7/29/2016

For I.J., who will not only help me find terrible disaster movies to watch for "research" but will find an ice cream that fits the theme.

Ray

The day of the disaster, everyone knew Harper was still furious.

She hadn't spoken to Ray, Liam, or Sasha since Friday night. Hadn't returned messages, hadn't accepted apologies. Now it was Monday—lunchtime. And Ray knew things were about to get ugly.

"Maybe she won't even sit here," said Sasha, as she parked her wheelchair at the end of their table. "Maybe she'll sit with Nina and Kailee today."

"And miss a chance to give us a hard time?" scoffed Ray. "Not likely. You know Harper."

They all knew Harper. Since elementary school, the four of them had stuck together. They all had other friends—even Harper, kind of. But who else knew that Liam had been in love with Tina Choi for three years? Who else could Ray talk to about his parents' daily arguments? Who else had camped out in Sasha's hospital room after the accident two years ago? Nobody. Each of them knew the others in ways no one else did.

Just like they all knew Harper had a limited capacity for silent sulking. Pretty soon she was going to explode. At them.

Sure enough, by the time Ray had popped open his bottle of water, Harper showed up.

Ray had left plenty of room for her, but she didn't take her seat. She just stood there, holding her lunch tray and glaring at her three closest friends.

"Are you still mad about Friday?" asked Liam. He'd never had any problem stating the obvious. After Sasha's accident two years ago, he'd literally said, *Guess it'll be awhile before you can walk, huh?*

"Of course—I'm still mad—about Friday." She bit off the words in angry chunks. "What, you thought I'd be over it?"

Ray held up his hands in a surrender pose. "Look, Harper, we're really sorry, seriously. And we've all said so, like, eighty times. What do you want us to do? If there's a way for us to make it up to you, tell us."

The way Ray remembered it, it had happened like this: Friday had been a warm day, even for the middle of May in central California. So after school, they'd all gone to Neptune Park with a few other people. Sasha's friend Chloe was there. And Drew, the guy Ray was sort of seeing. Drew had brought along Elissa and Max. Ray was pretty sure Liam's neighbor, Justin, had been there for a while too. Anyway, a big group of them had been hanging out at the park. Sasha and Harper had brought their cameras—the fancy cameras with shutter speeds and film and whatever. They had a photography class together and they were taking pictures for an assignment. The park was a good place for this because, according to Harper, it had texture. Ray had seen her snap pictures of the swing set, the links of the fence around the basketball court, the sand in the volleyball pit. Plus there were trees surrounding the park on three sides, and the Prospect Hotel stood at the northwest corner.

The hotel had been abandoned and condemned for years—which meant people spent way more time there now than when it was open for business. It had been built back in the 1850s, during the Gold Rush, so it had that old-timey elegant architecture: two floors, a wrap-around balcony on the second floor, a wide porch at ground level, lots of pillars. And, these days, lots of dirt and mold and cobwebs and other things that qualified as good "texture" for photos.

On Friday, Harper and Sasha had taken some photos while the rest of them played volleyball. Then Sasha started a rival game of basketball, since the sand in the volleyball pit could damage her wheelchair. Soon everyone had abandoned the sand for the asphalt court at the southern end of the park. Harper photographed the action for a while. Then she'd called, "I'll be right back—gonna grab some more photos of the hotel in this light."

About fifteen minutes later they'd wrapped up their game and walked to Drew's house a few blocks away. Drew had a huge backyard with a fire pit. And excellent speakers. And a wide range of beverages.

Flash forward half an hour to Ray looking down at his phone. By then he had eight missed calls, seventeen texts, and two Snapchat messages from Harper. Liam's and Sasha's phones told similar stories.

They'd forgotten about Harper. They'd left her at the park.

Ray called her back immediately. He even put her on speakerphone so Liam and Sasha could apologize with him. "We're at Drew's. We thought you were with us. We just didn't realize with the big group . . . " But Harper hung up on them and never showed up at Drew's.

Now, more than two days later, Ray had run out of ways to apologize.

But Harper hadn't run out of reasons to be angry.

"The damage is done," she was saying now. She sounded close to tears, but her expression was pure anger. "And I lost the keychain that night too."

The keychain was probably Harper's most prized possession. She kept it clipped to her camera case. It had belonged to her mom, who died when Harper was four. The keychain was nothing special to look at: a flat circle of metal shaped like a compass rose, with the four cardinal directions marked: N, S, E, W. But Harper loved it more than she loved the camera.

"Oh, man, Harper," Ray said quietly. "I'm sorry. Maybe it's still there . . . "

"I went back Saturday and looked for it. I couldn't find it. But that's not even what upsets me most. What really hurts is that you guys forgot about me."

"Harper, it was a mistake," said Liam. "We weren't, like, purposely ditching you. And it's not like we've ever lost track of you like that before. It definitely won't happen again. So what do you want from us?"

"I guess I just wonder if—I mean, if you didn't miss me then, maybe you wouldn't even notice if I stopped hanging out with you completely."

Ray shook his head. "Come on, Harper, you know that's not true."

"We're like a rhombus," said Liam. "All four sides are equally important."

Ray almost laughed. "Seriously, man? A rhombus?"

Harper didn't look amused *or* convinced. "But that's what I'm saying. I don't think I *am* equally important. You never would've forgotten Sasha."

The moment the words left her mouth, she froze. Ray felt himself stiffening too.

"Well," said Sasha quietly, "I'm kind of hard to miss. Lucky me."

"I didn't . . . " Harper stammered. "I didn't mean it like—"

"I know," Sasha cut her off. "But what *do* you mean, Harper? Do you mean you don't believe we care about you? Is that what you're trying to say?"

For a second Harper looked as if she might burst into tears. But then she snapped, "Maybe it is!"

Before any of them could respond, Harper turned and started speed-walking away from them. Ray watched her blonde head move toward the doors. She dropped her tray on a random table and left the cafeteria.

"Bet she's going to see your mom," said Liam to Sasha, whose mom was the school nurse. "With a 'migraine.'"

Sasha shot him a disapproving look. "Don't say it like that. Harper does get migraines."

"Yeah, but sometimes she just feels like going home early," said Liam. "When she just 'can't deal,' or whatever. Seriously, guys, isn't it starting to get old?"

"We did leave her behind," Sasha said, like anyone needed reminding. "And it was thoughtless of us. I understand why it ticked her off."

"Here's the thing, though," Liam pressed on. "Everything's a huge deal with her. She turns the smallest things into drama. Yeah, we probably wouldn't have left *you* behind, Sasha, but if we somehow had, would you hold a grudge over it? Would any of us get this worked up over an honest mistake?"

He's right, Ray thought. The rest of them all had other good friends. The rest of them all did things on their own. Harper didn't have any other *real* friends, and she hated being alone. So that left Ray, Liam, and Sasha to hang out with her, to support her. It got—not *old*, that wasn't the right way to put it. *Draining.* Feeling like whenever they weren't available, they were letting her down. Feeling like there was never a point when she didn't need something from at least one of them.

"Yeah," Ray agreed. "I mean, there's only so much we can do. She should know by now that we all love her and want her to be happy and yada yada. But, like, we also have our own lives. We didn't sign a contract that says we have to drop everything for her all the time.

And it's not fair for her to expect that from any of us."

"I just worry about her," murmured Sasha. "We've only got one year left of high school. What happens when we graduate? We're not all going to stay in Edson. We'll all do our own things, go our separate ways. What's Harper going to do then?"

"I think," said Ray carefully, "only Harper is responsible for that. We're her friends, but we can't always be her safety net."

Sasha nodded slowly. She, of all people, would have a hard time arguing with that. She'd never expected any of her friends to treat her differently after her accident. She'd never wanted special treatment or reassurance or protection. When people who'd never even spoken to her tried to be friendly or helpful, she appreciated it, but it also seemed to Ray that she felt weirded out. And when people who used to be friendly started avoiding her, she said "Their loss," and moved on.

"I still feel like crap, though," Sasha said. "I mean, knowing Harper's this upset, and knowing there's nothing else we can do about it . . ."

"Yeah," sighed Ray. He picked up his sandwich, suddenly realizing how hungry he was. "Well, on the plus side, the day probably won't get any worse."

On any other day, he would've been right.

But on that day, just a few hours later, the earthquake hit.

2

Sasha

Earthquakes were normal in California. The town of Edson sat right on top of a crack in the earth's crust, one of the mini fault lines that branched out from the San Andreas. Sasha had lost count of how many earthquakes she'd experienced. Most were just tiny blips on the Richter scale, lasting only a few seconds, barely rattling the coasters on the living room coffee table.

For most of her life, Sasha had practiced for earthquakes the "normal" way. During drills at school, she ducked under her desk and held on to the desk leg. When an earthquake struck at home, she dove under her kitchen table. Once, she'd woken up in the middle of the night, feeling her bed shaking up and down. She'd pulled her blankets over her head, to protect herself against falling objects, and waited it out.

That experience probably came closest to her current earthquake response strategy. Stay put, cover your head, and hope for the best. Being in the wheelchair had made her a little more nervous about earthquakes—about any emergency. She used to love disaster movies. She and Liam went to every summer blockbuster with a collapsing bridge in the trailer. They used to joke that if they were in one of these movies, they'd never make it through the first half hour. Since the accident, Sasha hadn't been so keen to see those films. Not just because the Edson movie theater was wheelchair accessible in name only. But because now, she knew that if she were a character in one of these movies, she'd be killed off within the first ten minutes. Or else the star would rescue her and tote her around like a ragdoll the whole time.

As for real-life disasters . . . for a while she'd thought about them obsessively. *What would I do if . . .* or *How would I get out of this building in the event of . . .* But then it had started to seem ridiculous. Real disasters happened so fast. The car that had hit her came out of nowhere. You couldn't plan your reaction ahead of time. You couldn't predict how things would play out.

Which left her with just the basics: stay put, cover your head, and hope for the best.

That's what she did at two o'clock that afternoon, when the earthquake hit.

***

Sasha, Liam, and Ray were in the library. They were supposed to be working on a presentation for English class and their English teacher had given them permission to do research in the library. The three of them sat at one of the tables in the open workspace at the back, near the windows, pretending to look through some books.

"Harper picked a good day to go home early," said Liam. "Independent research in

English, a substitute teacher in history—"

"Did you watch *The Last Days of Pompeii* again?" asked Ray.

"Obviously. That's what we always watch when Mr. Norman is out. I swear, that movie is *actually* three days long. I heard that one class did get to the part where the volcano erupts, but it was only because they lied to the substitute about where they left off."

"But it's the character development that matters . . . "

"There'll be algebra homework, though," Sasha cut in before Ray could get going on some nerdy lecture about cinematic storytelling strategies. "Worksheet due Monday. Do you think I should pick up an extra handout for Harper? Or just let her get one from Mrs. Oliver tomorrow?"

"Why does Mrs. Oliver still do worksheets anyway?" asked Liam. "Printed paper is so wasteful. Why can't we just do everything online?"

"You realize we're in a library," said Ray.

"Which just proves my point." Liam held

up the novel they'd been reading for class. "I guarantee you I can find this online. This is a 2012 reprint of a book that was published in 1844. Why did the world need this? How many trees died in 2012 for a book I can read on Project Gutenberg?"

"Guys," said Sasha. "I was asking your opinion about Harper."

Ray put his head on the table. Harper might be the most dramatic one, but Ray was the runner-up. "I literally can't devote another brain cell to Harper today. If you can, Sasha, good for you."

That's when the floor started to shake.

Actually, everything started to shake. A low rumbling noise filled the air. No one needed to ask what was going on. They all knew the drill. Liam and Ray disappeared under the table. Sasha backed her wheelchair against the wall, locked the wheels, and curled her upper body into a fetal position.

Instinctively, Sasha started counting the seconds. Three—four—five—

She heard books topple off their shelves

and hit the floor with a scattered drumbeat noise. Luckily the bookcases themselves were nailed to the floor, and their rows ended just where the table workspace began. But even though Sasha was parked in a bookshelf-free space, several books struck her arms, which she'd raised to cover her head. Liam was right. Digital was the way to go.

Ten seconds, eleven—*Man, this is a long one . . .*

Sasha heard the windows shatter. She didn't feel any glass hit her, though, and she prayed that none had lodged in her wheelchair tires.

Fifteen seconds—

Her wheelchair was moving. Even though the brakes were on, the wheels hopped forward and back, forward and back, in sickening little jolts. That's what she got for having an ultra-light manual wheelchair, instead of a powerchair that weighed as much as a tank. *Don't tip over, don't tip over . . .* Sasha was starting to feel nauseated, as if she were on a rollercoaster.

Twenty seconds—

And then stillness.

3

Harper

It was dark. And hard to breathe.

You have to breathe. Come on, you have to breathe.

Okay, fine, she was breathing. The air was thick with dust and dirt particles, but she was breathing. As one desperate thought faded, another took its place.

How could you be so stupid? No one even knows you're here.

4

Sasha

The fire alarm was going off. It kept a shrill beat, echoing off the cinderblock walls of the school.

Slowly, Sasha lowered her arms and sat up straight.

She wasn't anywhere near the wall anymore. Her chair had drifted into the middle of the room.

To her right, toward the windows, glass shards covered the floor.

To her left, piles of fallen books sat in front of empty shelves. Study tables had slid against bookcases. A large potted plant had tipped over in front of library's double doors. Ms. Midio, the librarian, shouted, "Someone call 9-1-1!" Sasha couldn't actually see Ms. Midio—she just heard her urgent voice.

Liam and Ray crawled out from under their table in front of Sasha. Their chairs—and the books they'd spread on the table—now lay on the floor several feet away.

"That was crazy," gasped Ray. "I don't think I've ever felt a quake that big."

"You okay, Sasha?" Liam called over the bellowing fire alarm.

"As far as I can tell, yeah." She reached down and unlocked her wheels. They looked okay—no obvious punctures.

Ms. Midio was still shouting. "Is someone calling 9-1-1? Can anyone hear me? Answer me, please!"

"On it!" shouted Sasha, pulling her phone out of her jeans pocket. "Are you okay, Ms. Midio?"

"I—I've hit my head, I think."

Liam stood up. "Where are you?" he called. "We can't see you."

"Behind the front desk. A—part of a light—fell from the ceiling—"

Liam rushed toward the front of the library, climbing around overturned chairs and spilled books. Ray moved closer to Sasha and pulled out his own phone.

Sasha had never called 9-1-1 before. She'd been in no shape to do it when she needed it two years ago. Someone else—the driver who hit her—had made the call. Still, dialing the numbers made her think of the intersection of Pleasant Street and Miles Avenue. She swallowed the sour taste in the back of her throat.

The 9-1-1 dispatcher's voice came through her phone, asking the nature of her emergency. "Hi, yeah, I'm at Garrison High School, in the library, and someone was hit in the head during the earthquake, possibly by a falling light fixture . . . "

"Is she conscious?" the dispatcher asked immediately.

"Yes—"

"We'll get someone over there as soon as

we can. Response time is going to be slower than usual because of debris blocking some of the streets and because of the huge need right now."

"Okay, I understand. Should I hang up so you can answer more calls?"

"We'd appreciate that."

Sasha ended the call. By now, Liam was almost at the front desk. "Ms. Midio, help is one the way," he said.

"Don't try to move her," Sasha called to him. "Especially her head." As the daughter of the school nurse, she'd picked up on some first aid tips here and there.

"Just stay still, Ms. Midio," Liam said. He disappeared behind the front desk. Sasha couldn't see him anymore, but she could still hear him. "Here, I'll get that off you . . . Better? Yeah, just stay right there—"

"I'm all right. I can sit up," Ms. Midio groaned.

"Uh, okay, just take it easy. Great, okay, now just sit like that for a minute. Help will be here soon."

The principal's voice came on over the PA system. It was hard to hear her with the fire alarm still buzzing, but Sasha managed to get the gist of the announcement.

" . . . Teachers need to evacuate the school immediately . . . Gather in the parking lot . . . Need to stay calm . . . Proceed in an orderly fashion . . . "

Ray moved toward the windows, stepping around the bigger shards of glass. "People are already pouring out the front doors," he reported.

"Do you see my mom?" asked Sasha.

Ray shook his head. "She's not jumping out at me. Too many people. We'd better get out there."

Up at the front of the library, Ms. Midio was saying, "I'm fine, I'm fine now, really." She stood up, and Sasha finally saw her. She wasn't bleeding, but her hair was mussed and her expression seemed a little dazed. Liam grabbed her arm to steady her.

"Okay, Ms. Midio," Liam said. "If you think you can walk, let's get you outside.

Then you're gonna sit down and wait for the paramedics. Got it?"

She nodded.

"All right, let's go." He turned toward Ray and Sasha. "I'll be right back, guys."

"No, we'll meet you outside," said Sasha. Standard earthquake procedure: you're not supposed to go back into a building after you've exited.

But Sasha wasn't sure Liam heard her over the blare of the fire alarm. Plus he was focused on keeping Ms. Midio upright and on moving the giant fallen plant away from the door.

In her mind, Sasha traced a path from her current position to the library doors. As a little kid, she'd run obstacle courses in gym class. Now, she saw most of the world as an obstacle course. She'd learned to dodge stairs, curbs, steep drops, sections of sidewalk pushed up by tree roots.

But this was on a whole other level.

Ray was already starting to clear a path for her, shoving tables and chairs and books out of the way. Sasha wheeled herself forward, a half-turn at a time. *Don't be impatient. Impatience gets you nowhere.* That was one of the first lessons she'd learned after her accident.

Still, she couldn't keep her heart rate from kicking up a few notches. Garrison High School had been built to follow the state's earthquake codes, which meant it should be able to withstand a powerful quake. But it had also been built in the 1990s, and Sasha's mom was always complaining that the building needed more upgrades than the school system could afford.

Sasha didn't want to stick around to find out how badly the building needed those upgrades.

5

Liam

The power was out. Liam didn't realize it until he stepped into the hallway and registered how dim it was. The fire alarm was still pulsing. It was starting to give him a headache, actually.

His priorities: One, get Ms. Midio outside and turn her over to a responsible adult. Ideally Mrs. Hill, Sasha's mom. Two, make sure Sasha and Ray got out okay. Liam knew he shouldn't go back inside the building once he was out. Year after year, they'd all heard the same safety tips during their drills at school. But Liam didn't like leaving his friends to fend for themselves, either.

The hallway in front of him led directly to the front doors of the school. Liam and Ms. Midio were only about fifty yards away from the freedom of the outdoors. The hallway was empty. Most of the other students and staff must've evacuated already.

Correction: the hallway was empty, except for the massive chunk of the ceiling that had fallen into the middle of the floor.

Liam stared at the huge piece of concrete in his path. Wires hung from the hole in the ceiling, limp and sad, like skinny arms reaching helplessly toward the concrete.

"Ohhhhkay," he said to Ms. Midio. "We're just gonna walk around that *really carefully*. Watch your step, Ms. Midio."

Even with Ms. Midio a little unsteady on her feet, it wasn't hard to sidestep the danger zone. Liam hugged the wall and stepped cautiously over smaller pieces of broken concrete. He held his breath, trying not to inhale the dirt particles floating in the air. Half a second later, he and Ms. Midio were clear of the rubble. Still, he didn't feel any better.

There's no way Sasha can get past that.

The rest of the hallway seemed to be intact. They had a clear path to the front entrance now. Liam picked up the pace, moving as fast as Ms. Midio seemed comfortable with. He shoved open a door and walked out into the sunlight, leaving the screech of the fire alarm behind.

Students milled around in the parking lot, hugging or searching for their friends. Teachers frantically tried to keep their classes together and take head counts. Liam didn't see a single emergency vehicle.

He spotted Sasha's mom sitting on the sidewalk curb with a crying freshman.

"Mrs. Hill!" he called to her. "Ms. Midio hit her head. We think she might have a concussion. Can you keep an eye on her?"

"Liam! Of course. Where's Sasha?"

"She's fine," Liam told her, already turning around.

"But where—"

"Hold that thought, Mrs. Hill."

Before anyone could stop him, he sprinted back into the school.

6

Sasha

Ray and Sasha had almost reached the library doors when Liam reappeared. "Hey! I don't think you're gonna be able to get through the hallway, Sasha. Part of the ceiling fell in."

Ray's eyes widened. *"Part of the ceiling fell in?* And you took the risk of coming back inside? What were you thinking?"

"One, I wanted to warn you. And two, obviously I'm an idiot. Moving on."

Sasha waved her hand, signaling him to step aside. "Let me through. I want to see."

Liam moved out of her way. She wheeled herself forward, into the hallway.

There was a crater in the ceiling. The fallen debris and the dangling wires added up to a five-foot-high pile of *you-shall-not-pass*.

"Okay, you're right, Liam." She hated saying it, hated admitting defeat. Mostly, she hated the thought of being stuck here until an emergency crew showed up, while everyone else rushed outside . . .

"We'll stay with you till the emergency crews get here," said Ray.

Sasha glanced away, grateful for how casually he made the offer—and knowing she shouldn't accept it.

"Sooo, do you have a plan for what to do if the rest of the ceiling falls on us?" asked Liam. "Because we probably won't be much help to Sasha if we let ourselves get trapped inside a collapsed building."

"Says the guy who got outside and chose to come back in," muttered Ray.

Liam ignored that comment. "We can get her out another way. There are side doors, emergency exits, aren't there? Somewhere?"

"Yeah, but I don't think it's a great idea to go wandering around in building with an unstable roof."

"We don't know for sure that the rest of the roof is unstable—"

"And I'd rather not find out!"

While Ray and Liam bickered, Sasha's eyes drifted back into the library, to the table where they'd been sitting a minute ago. Sunlight poured through the shattered windows.

Wait.

"Guys, what if we don't use the hallway?" Sasha said. "What if we use the library window instead?"

"Uh," said Liam, "how exactly are you going to climb out of a window, Sasha?"

Good old Liam, always needing it spelled out for him. "With help," she said.

***

Sasha loved her wheelchair. It had a rigid frame, which meant it didn't fold up like the wheelchair her great-grandma used. But it was small and ultra-light, and the wheels detached.

Sasha was used to getting herself in and out of it—every morning and night, every time she went to the bathroom, every time she got into a car. But even with her strong arms, great balance, and years of experience, she knew she couldn't get herself out of the library window on her own. The windowsill was just too high.

That was where Liam and Ray came in.

By now, they knew her wheelchair almost as well as she did. They called it Peg—short for Pegasus, the flying horse from Greek mythology. Ray's idea, because Ray was the nerd of all nerds. And just as important, they understood Peg the Wheelchair's relationship with Sasha. So they knew exactly what to do.

Liam started by carefully lifting Sasha out of the chair. (It helped that Liam was built like a retired linebacker. His muscles might not have been rock solid, but he had enough bulk to support plenty of weight easily.) Meanwhile, Ray used his spiral notebook to sweep a path through the broken glass on the floor and to clear the shards off the windowsill and frame.

Next, Ray popped the wheels off the chair so that he could easily pass each piece of Peg through the window. He leaned down over the windowsill and lowered each piece carefully to the grass on the other side before climbing through himself. Then, he carried the pieces to the smooth blacktop of the parking lot, where he quickly reassembled the chair.

Back inside, Liam sat down on the window sill, holding Sasha against his chest. Bracing his back against the window frame, he swung one of his legs over, then the other. By the time he carried Sasha into the parking lot, Ray had her chariot ready.

They heard a rumble and then a crash somewhere nearby.

Liam jumped. "What was that?"

"I think it was another part of the roof," said Ray. "Dude, it was such a bad idea for you to go back inside. I mean, we could get hit with an aftershock at any time. And who knows what could happen to the roof then?"

Aftershocks always followed big quakes. They were basically spin-off earthquakes—less powerful echoes of the main event. Sometimes they came a few hours later. Sometimes they went on for days, weeks, even months. They tended to get a little weaker each time, so at a certain point they weren't worth worrying about anymore.

That point hadn't arrived yet.

Often, aftershocks caused more damage than the original quake, giving weakened structures the extra whack they were waiting for. Garrison High School looked as if the slightest nudge might collapse it.

"You're welcome," said Liam sarcastically to Ray. "No need to throw me a parade. I just didn't feel comfortable leaving my friends behind when they could be in danger, that's all. Hold your applause."

Ray sighed. "Okay, I probably would've done the same thing. But it was still stupid."

"Duly noted, Grandma."

Just then, Mrs. Hill came running over. "Sasha! Oh, honey, are you okay? I was keeping an eye on the ramp, but I never saw you come out."

"Yeah," Sasha smiled innocently. "That's because I didn't use the ramp. I couldn't get out through the main entrance."

"Then how did you get out?"

"Oh, you know, just some blockbuster stunts."

Liam jumped in. "Is Ms. Midio okay, Mrs. Hill?"

Mrs. Hill turned to him. "She's going to be fine. Possibly a mild concussion, but nothing too serious. I have Mrs. Oliver watching her. *You*, young man—"

"I know, I know, bad life choices."

Mrs. Hill turned back to her daughter and shook her head. "I'm glad you're out of there, but I hope you didn't do anything too risky. You could've damaged your chair, even if you didn't hurt yourself."

"Chair and I are both fine," Sasha assured her. She never called the chair Peg in front of her mom. Changing the subject, she asked, "What about Jeremiah, though?" Sasha's little brother went the elementary school a few blocks from the Hills' house. That school was newer than Garrison High, so Sasha hoped its roof was sturdier.

Mrs. Hill's face was always stretched thin over a sea of suppressed worries. But at the moment, it looked even more strained than usual. "I don't know. I can't get any calls through. The cell towers are probably jammed. That can happen in an emergency situation. And I tried to text Mattie"—that was the elementary school's vice principal—"but that didn't go through either."

They heard the principal's voice again. This time it came from the megaphone she was holding, instead of from the internal PA system. "Students! Students, I need your attention, please! Clap once if you can hear me."

"Oh, come on . . ." muttered Ray in irritation. But he clapped anyway.

After the successful "clap twice" stage of the exercise, the principal continued. "Emergency responders will be arriving soon. Anyone who needs medical attention should see Mrs. Hill in the meantime. School is canceled for the rest of the day."

"What about our stuff?" yelled a student.

"Yeah, my backpack's still inside!" someone else added.

"It's not safe to reenter the building," the principal said. "But your items will be returned to you as soon as possible. Meanwhile, I encourage you to stay here until you can contact your families. You should wait to return home until building managers confirm that your homes are safe. I urge you to be extremely careful. Many buildings may be damaged. And of course we have to be prepared for aftershocks. Be smart, and be safe."

"Easier said than done," said Sasha under her breath as the principal lowered her megaphone. Students immediately started murmuring among themselves. No one seemed any calmer than before the principal had spoken.

"How are we supposed to contact our families if we can't get calls or texts to go through?" demanded Liam. He sounded personally offended that the principal hadn't thought of this.

Ray studied his phone screen. "Hold on . . . Yeah, okay, my phone is still connected to the Internet. So I'm just gonna e-mail my parents. This would be easier if they knew how to send messages through phone apps, but I mean . . . old people."

"We should check in with Harper while we're at it," said Sasha.

"Good idea," said Liam, whipping out his own phone. "Just sent her a Facebook message."

"Sasha, honey, will you be okay here while I take care of some kids' bumps and bruises?" Mrs. Hill asked. "We'll head home as soon as the ambulances get here."

For the next fifteen minutes, Sasha waited. Waited for an aftershock, which didn't come. Waited for news, hopping from site to site on her phone. Her brother's school's Twitter account announced that everyone was okay and that kids were waiting outside to be picked up. The town's official website said that the Edson Community Center would be open to citizens who'd had to evacuate their homes. Other friends drifted over—checking in, offering hugs, comparing stories. Ray and Liam heard back from their parents, who were stuck at work but unhurt. Sasha sent her own message to Harper, but she didn't hear anything. Liam didn't hear from Harper either. Ray finally tried too, with no results.

"She's probably just still sulking about Friday," said Ray. "I'm sure she's fine."

"But even Harper wouldn't give us the silent treatment after an *earthquake*, would she?"

"Maybe she just hasn't checked her phone," Liam suggested.

But Sasha couldn't help it. A sharp twinge of uneasiness ran through all the parts of her body that still had feeling in them. Either Harper wasn't answering their messages because she truly was that ticked off, or she wasn't answering because she *couldn't*.

The second possibility was more worrying, but the first one was upsetting too.

Because yeah, Harper was clingy. She was dramatic. She could be, in some ways, immature. But it was Harper who had created a funny new meme to send to Sasha every morning that Sasha spent in the hospital. It was Harper who baked something amazing for every birthday. It was Harper who would listen to you talk for hours, or just sit in silence with you for the same amount of time. She was a caring, fun, generous friend. She was more of a giver than a taker. And that made it hard for Sasha to stop thinking about Harper's face at lunch today. From one angle, sure, Harper was overreacting. But from another angle—she would bend over backwards for any one of them and they had let her down on Friday.

Maybe they could all chip in to buy her a new keychain to replace the treasured one she'd lost. Maybe that was the symbolic making-amends gesture that Harper needed.

Part of Sasha wanted to assume that Harper would get over this. But part of her knew that friendships got ruined for less-important reasons all the time. She didn't want to lose Harper as a friend just because she and Liam and Ray couldn't find a way to assure Harper that she mattered to them.

On the other hand, it was hard to be too concerned about Harper's feelings when Sasha was even more concerned about Harper's *safety*.

"News sites are saying the quake was a six-point-five on the Richter scale," Ray reported, his eyes glued to his phone. "That's intense."

"Well, yeah, it *felt* intense," Liam pointed out.

"I mean, that's the most severe earthquake to hit this area in our lifetime."

Liam nodded thoughtfully. "Man, the aftershocks are gonna be huge."

Sasha

An ambulance and a fire truck finally pulled up in the school parking lot. Mrs. Hill helped guide a few people, including Ms. Midio, over to the paramedics. Then she returned to Sasha, Liam, and Ray. "Ready to get out of here, honey?"

"Is it safe to go home?" asked Sasha.

"I don't know yet. We're not supposed to go back until we hear from city authorities. So I figure I'll drop you off at the community center, where they've got the emergency shelter set up, and then go get Jeremiah."

Sasha glanced worriedly at Liam and Ray. Ray's parents both worked in Davis, an hour away. Liam's mom was all the way in Sacramento, which was almost a two-hour drive. With road damage and post-disaster traffic, it could take them all day to get back to Edson. Sasha didn't like the idea of ditching her friends in the school parking lot. "We'll be fine," Ray told her, clearly reading her mind. "We can always just walk to the community center."

"Yeah." Liam nodded. "There should be food there, at least."

"Why don't I just give you boys a ride there?" asked Mrs. Hill.

Two minutes later, they were all inside the Hills' car. Ray and Liam helped disassemble and store Sasha's wheelchair after she transferred into the front passenger's seat, so they were ready to go in record time.

"Thanks for this, Mrs. Hill," said Liam as Sasha's mom steered around the fire truck to exit the parking lot.

"No problem," she replied.

Except, as it turned out, it *was* kind of a problem.

The streets were in bad shape. A power line lay across Holland Avenue, so Mrs. Hill had to detour to Carpenter Street. But the light was out at the intersection, forcing cars to move in a nervous start-stop-look-okay-now-go dance. Fallen trees blocked part of Altatierra Street. A water main had burst on Phoenix Drive. Sasha didn't see a lot of damage to buildings, but everything else was a mess. Twice, Mrs. Hill had to pull over to let emergency vehicles race past her.

After the fifth or sixth detour, Mrs. Hill said, "Guys, I don't think it's safe for me to be driving at this point. I'm not sure I can get us all the way to the community center. I'll be lucky if I get as far as our house."

They did get as far as the Hills' house, and it didn't seem damaged: no broken windows, no obvious missing pieces. Sasha and the boys stayed in the car while Mrs. Hill checked it out. When she came back, she reported, "Nothing's on fire. I didn't smell gas. And the walls and ceiling seem stable—and if they're not, I'll sue that contractor. I think we'd better call it quits and stay here."

"That's fine, Mrs. Hill," said Ray quickly. "Liam and I can walk the rest of the way to the community center. You've gotten us a lot closer, at least."

"You're welcome to hang out at our house until things settle down a little," Mrs. Hill offered.

"Thanks, but we wouldn't want to be in the way," Ray said. "I'm sure you'll have a lot of cleanup to do."

"Can you stop by Harper's house on your way to the community center?" Sasha asked the boys. "Just to make sure she's all right? Since none of us have heard back from her."

Liam nodded. "Definitely."

Mrs. Hill was frowning, but she said, "All right. Just be careful. Can you send Sasha a message when you get to the community center so we know everything's all right?"

"For sure," said Ray.

"Couldn't I go with them?" Sasha asked her mom. "At least as far as Harper's? Just to—"

"Absolutely not!" said Mrs. Hill. "The sidewalks will be a warzone."

Sasha knew this was completely reasonable. But she was also tempted to curl her hands into fists and punch her legs. It wasn't as if she'd feel anything if she did.

"I could use my mountain bike wheels . . . " For her last birthday, her uncle had gotten her a pair of hardcore shock-absorbing tires. Compared to her usual tires, they were way sturdier and less likely to puncture. Sasha used them for most of her outdoor activities now.

"Still no," said her mother firmly. "There'll be aftershocks. And I need your help getting the house back in shape."

Sasha bit the inside of her cheek. Her family was really good about not telling her to sit in a corner and rest. They encouraged her to be independent. And like her friends, they treated her like part of a team, not like someone who had to be helped and protected all the time. But still—*I need your help getting the house back in shape?* How was she supposed to take that seriously? As if sweeping the kitchen floor was on par with confirming someone's safety.

"Message me as soon as you get to Harper's," she told Liam and Ray. "I'll feel a lot better once I know she's okay."

"We all will," said Liam grimly.

8

Liam

Harper's house was five blocks away from Sasha's, but even in that short distance, the damage level seemed to spike. This part of the neighborhood might as well have been hit with a wrecking ball. Trees were down, power lines slanted dangerously. Liam saw a garage that had folded sideways like a collapsible cardboard box. Porch rails had buckled, pieces of roofs had collapsed, windows had blown out.

The neighborhood was also weirdly quiet.

Liam almost missed the unending fire alarm at school. Somewhere off in the distance he heard sirens, but he found himself wishing they were closer. It would be nice to know that help was nearby if they needed it.

Liam wasn't sure he wanted to see his own house—or Harper's.

He and Ray had been to Harper's house hundreds of times. The first time was probably in kindergarten, when everyone in the class had been invited to Harper's birthday party. That was Harper's first birthday without her mom. She'd hugged everyone who came, even the boys. And she made sure everybody else got a piece of cake before she started eating.

Weird thing to think about now. Almost like the kind of story you'd tell at someone's funeral.

You idiot, he said sternly to himself. *She's fine. I'm sure she's fine.*

When they got to the house, he let out a giant exhale. It was fine. At least it looked fine from the outside.

Liam and Ray rushed up to the front door, and Ray rang the bell. Harper's dad's car wasn't in the driveway. He was probably still at his office in Sacramento. But Harper should've been here.

They waited five seconds before Ray pushed the doorbell again. They heard it echoing inside the house—but still no answer.

"Harper?" called Liam. "Are you there?" Silence. "Are you okay? We just wanted to make sure you're okay. You don't have to talk to us otherwise. We're just worried."

More silence.

"Harper!" Ray shouted. He banged on the door with his fist. "Quit being stupid! We're calling 9-1-1 if you don't at least yell to us that you're okay."

For a split second, Liam really did expect to hear her voice: *Leave me alone! Just forget about me. You're good at that.*

But that didn't happen.

Ray pounded more forcefully on the door. "Harper! ARE YOU OKAY?"

"Ray." Liam grabbed his friend's arm before the door got dented. "I don't think she's here."

Ray turned toward him, looking as if he'd lost his balance, even though the earth was holding steady for the moment. "But she left

school three hours ago. If she's not here—
where is she?"

Liam could only shake his head. "I
don't know."

9

Harper

She couldn't reach her phone. She couldn't move, period. One arm was stuck above her head. The other was pinned to her side.

But what good would her phone do her anyway? So many people would be making emergency calls that the cell towers would be swamped.

She could try yelling for help.

As if any emergency responders would come *here* first. As if anyone would think to check this place. Plus, she was pretty sure it was a bad idea to take super-deep breaths. All kinds of toxins could be leaking into the air, rising out of the debris.

Lying here in the dark, Harper realized this was exactly what she'd been afraid of ever since her mom died.

Being left alone and knowing nobody was coming for her.

10

Sasha

Sasha's mom was working hard to clear a path for her. Everything in their living room had either fallen over or shifted position, as if an angry ghost had decided to redecorate the house. "Power hasn't gone out, so the fridge should be working fine," her mom said over her shoulder. "But a lot of food spilled out onto the floor during the quake, so we might have to toss some of it. Everything in the closets has probably shifted too. I'll probably need to clean up some spills."

"And where do I come in?" Sasha asked pointedly. "In terms of helping you?"

"I'll let you know once I've assessed the damage, honey."

Sasha bit her tongue as her mom left the room. She hated the phrase "assess the damage." Mostly because, two years ago, people had used it to talk about *her*: the damage to her legs, the damage to her life, the reasons she wouldn't be able to pick up a framed picture lying on the floor right in front of her. Assessing *that* damage was an ongoing process. And for the most part, it didn't make Sasha angry anymore. But it was frustrating, at moments like this, that she couldn't dive right in and help. She had to wait for a task that was within arm's reach.

Sasha felt her phone buzz.

It was Liam, calling her through a video chat app. This was the app they all used to call Ray when he was visiting family in Mexico. Ray and Liam might as well be in Mexico right now. Sasha had rarely felt farther away from them.

She accepted the call, and her phone screen filled with a blurry image of Liam's face. Judging by the moving background, she figured he was walking as he made the call. And judging by his expression, he didn't have good news to report.

"Hey! How's Harper?"

"Missing in action," said Liam. "Her house was fine, but nobody was there. She must've gone somewhere else after she left school."

Sasha fought to hold her phone steady. "And nobody knows where she is."

"Well, maybe her dad knows. We haven't tried getting in touch with him."

"I'll e-mail him right now," said Sasha. "Are you two still heading to the community center?"

"Yeah," said Liam.

"No," said Ray, off camera, at the same time.

Liam did a double take. "Uh—Ray? What's that supposed to mean?"

"I'm stopping by my apartment first," Sasha heard Ray say matter-of-factly. "It's on the way. I just want to see if it's damaged."

"Hold on, Ray—" Sasha said.

Liam talked over her. "That might be dangerous."

"I just want to *know*!" Ray snapped. "You don't have to come with me, Liam. You can go straight to the community center and have a doughnut."

"One, that's not fair," said Liam, starting off into his usual list of points. "This isn't about free doughnuts. You gave me a hard time earlier for going back into the school building and I wouldn't be a real friend if I didn't give you a hard time for *your* stupid decisions. Two, obviously I'm not letting you go there alone."

Sasha bit her lip. Usually she didn't feel like this. Usually her friends didn't *let* her feel like this. They always included her, let her contribute. But there was nothing she could do to help them right now.

Nothing she could do to help Harper, if Harper was in trouble.

She didn't hate her legs very often anymore. She'd learned to accept them, to not need them most of the time. But today was an exception. In her head, she insulted her legs pretty brutally.

"Be careful, you guys," she said to Liam's face on her phone screen.

Liam sighed. "Yeah, I'll work on that. And I'll call you back the next chance I get."

***

Sasha had finished e-mailing Harper's dad and had sent one more last-ditch text to Harper by the time her mom came back into the living room. "Okay," said Mrs. Hill, exhaling. "Things are looking pretty good. No sewage line issues—the toilet's flushing fine. I mopped up the worst of the spills. Nothing's on fire."

"All reassuring," said Sasha.

"I'm going to run over to the elementary school and get Jeremiah. Be back in twenty minutes."

"Okay, be safe." That was how they always ended conversations. At least it had been for the past two years. It had become their version of *I love you*.

And it felt especially appropriate today.

"Send me a message if anything comes up while I'm gone." Sasha's mom kissed her on the cheek as she headed past her. By the time Mrs. Hill had closed and locked the front door behind her, Sasha's phone buzzed. A new e-mail had just landed in her inbox.

It was from Harper's dad: *No, I haven't heard anything from Harper today. Now I'm getting worried.*

Harper

She wished she hadn't gotten so angry at her friends. It seemed so petty now. She wished she could tell them she forgave them—and ask them to forgive her for being such a child about the whole thing. She wished she could thank them for all the times they had been there for her, for all the ways they'd made her life awesome.

Her dad would blame himself for this, probably. She wished she could tell him not to.

Are you serious? What is WRONG with you?

She wasn't going to die here—not without

at least making an effort to survive. She needed to snap out of it.

And find a way to let someone know she was here.

12

Ray

"This is such a bad idea," said Liam for at least the fifth time as he and Ray climbed the stairs in Ray's apartment building. Ray knew he was bending the terms of their bargain. First it *was* *I just want to see the building and check that it's still standing.* Now it was *I just want to see inside the apartment.*

He knew Liam was right. From the outside, the building had looked fine. But with five stories, almost anything could go wrong at any minute.

Still, Ray couldn't turn back without seeing inside his apartment. Like he'd told Sasha and

Liam: he had to *know*. He needed to feel as if he was in control of something.

Because if Harper wasn't at home, where was she? And if she was hurt—or worse—how was he going to live with that? How could he ever forgive himself for saying that Harper's life wasn't their responsibility?

He couldn't do anything about that right now. What he could do was check out his apartment.

Ray and Liam reached the fifth floor and wheezed their way out of the stairwell. It wasn't safe to try the elevator right after an earthquake. Even if the building's power was working, the elevator could be damaged in other ways. And an elevator wasn't exactly a prime place to be during an aftershock—which could hit at any moment.

Ray ran down the hallway to his door. He fumbled for the key ring in his pocket and let himself in.

The apartment looked as if someone had trashed it. Like those spy movies where the main character comes home and realizes his cover is blown because the bad guys have torn apart his whole pad. The freestanding mini-bookcase had fallen over. The doors of the game cabinet stood open, its contents spilled onto the floor. The walls—normally covered in framed photos—were almost bare. The photos had dropped down to join the rest of the clutter on the floor. Ray halfheartedly scanned the floor for his parents' wedding picture, the one he often looked at to remind himself they'd been happy together once.

He picked his way through the mess to the kitchen. The fridge and freezer doors were open, spewing cold air. Cans and bottles had flown off the pantry shelves and smashed on the tile floor. Ray knelt down and started picking them up. He didn't know what else to do.

"You don't need to deal with all this right away, man," said Liam quietly. "Let's just go to the community center for now. You can worry about this when your parents get back."

Ray shook his head, but he also stood up again. He felt completely at a loss.

Suddenly he lurched forward—so fast he almost lost his balance completely. Before he could steady himself, gravity seemed to change its mind, jerking him backward.

Over the rumble of the earth shaking, Liam shouted, "It's an aftershock!"

Ray

Ray and Liam both ended up under the kitchen table. Each of them clung to a table leg as the floor vibrated beneath them. The aftershock felt almost as powerful as the main quake, and it definitely lasted almost as long. Ray counted thirteen seconds.

Cans and bottles rolled across the kitchen floor, banging into Ray's legs. He was prepared for that.

He *wasn't* prepared for the ceiling fan to crash to the floor about a foot from where he was crouched.

As the fan landed, Ray heard a high-pitched

shattering noise and a lower, deeper crunch. The fan's blades turned just slightly, as if a faint breeze was blowing them.

Over the rumbling noise of the actual quake, Ray heard everything his family owned jostling, cracking, groaning under the pressure of this powerful tremor.

When it was over, Ray and Liam climbed out from under the table. Ray stared down at the ceiling fan.

"Ray."

How are we going to fix all this? he thought. *Everything's ruined. Where do we even start?*

"Ray!"

Ray finally looked up at Liam.

"The walls are leaning, Ray. The whole *building* is leaning. Don't you see it?"

Ray squinted at a wall. It did look more slanted than usual.

Liam grabbed him by the shoulders. "Listen, man, we need to get out of here! Now!"

Ray knew Liam was right. And yet he couldn't make himself move. Was this how Sasha felt all the time?

Probably not. Because there was nothing actually wrong with Ray's legs. Liam proved this by dragging him into the living room.

Ray felt a switch flip inside his brain and suddenly he was able to focus again. "Okay, come on, we'll take the fire escape."

"Why—" Liam started to ask.

"Closer than the stairs," said Liam as he led them to the living room window. "And we can't trust the elevator."

The window glass hadn't held up well against two earthquakes. Ray found a dishcloth lying on the floor and used it to wipe down the sill. Then he climbed out onto the fire escape's scaffolding, with Liam right behind him.

The sound of the earthquake was gone, but Ray heard a new sound now. A sort of deep groan, as if the whole building was alive and on the verge of puking. Ray clattered down the first flight of fire-escape steps.

He smelled smoke in the air, but he didn't think it was close by. Another flight of steps— they were at the third floor landing now, dashing across the landing to the next set of stairs.

Was the building starting to shake? Or was the fire escape just rickety? Had to be the fire escape. The scaffolding rattled under Ray's pounding feet, sending shock waves through the rest of the metal structure.

Ray focused on the ground below. The fire escape was attached to the back of the building, where there was a small parking lot for residents. Ray was relieved to see only a few cars in the lot. That meant hardly anybody was in the building.

Aside from him and Liam.

Ray gripped the railing, but his palm was slick with sweat. He was taking the steps at a run now. He had barely started down the second-to-last set of stairs when his foot slipped.

In his head he saw the fallen ceiling fan, its blades moving in broken confusion. For some reason his brain jumped to that image, instead of picturing his own legs in a twisted heap or his own skull split open.

Liam grabbed him before he fell. He only missed one step. "Easy—you okay?" panted Liam.

"Yeah, thanks." Ray grabbed the railing with both hands and kept moving.

Okay, no: it wasn't just the fire escape that was shaking. Something was wrong with the building. It felt as if a shiver was passing through the whole structure.

One more floor to go. They'd reached the ladder that hung straight down over the final drop. Ray swung himself onto it, forced himself to take one rung at a time. When he reached the bottom rung, about five feet off the ground, he jumped the rest of the way.

Liam landed right behind him and grabbed Ray's arm. "*Run!*"

Behind them, the building's groan changed to a roar. Ray sprinted across the parking lot without looking back.

He slowed down when he reached the alley at the end of the parking lot. Liam wheezed to a stop and looked over his shoulder. Then he breathed a long, stretched-out sigh, half in horror, half in awe.

Ray pulled in several deep breaths. Yeah, he did smell smoke. But as he'd thought, it was far away.

He braced himself and turned around to see the damage.

His apartment building had sunk about twenty feet into the ground. The entire first floor had disappeared. The rest of the structure sat at a dramatic slant, leaning at almost a forty-five degree angle.

They stood there, trying to catch their breath. Ray lifted his hands to the top of his head while Liam bent forward, resting his hands on his knees. Ray felt his phone buzz in his pocket. It was a notification. "Hey," he said. "I think I've got service again."

Liam spent a few more seconds panting while Ray called 9-1-1.

14

Harper

The aftershock had dislodged something above her. One of her arms had a little wriggle room now.

Slowly, slowly she worked that arm toward her jeans pocket, where her phone was. Carefully she teased the phone out. She still wouldn't be able to get the phone to a spot where she could see it. She'd have to do her best with just her sense of touch.

First, she held down the power button. She felt it buzz as it turned off. Good—it wasn't broken. Or at least not completely broken. She turned it back on. For the first time in her life, she regretted having a touchscreen phone. Her dad's old-school phone with the actual buttons would've been much easier to work with.

At least there was no lock on her phone. All she had to do was touch the correct icon on her home screen. But if she hit the wrong icon, or just missed entirely, she'd be stuck. There'd be no way for her to figure out what she'd done wrong or where she'd ended up. She could always start over from scratch, but her phone hadn't been fully charged when she left school. No telling how many times she'd be able to repeat this process, hoping that she'd get it right at least once, before her phone died on her.

She'd have to make every attempt count.

She closed her eyes and thought about her phone screen. The texting icon was in the lower right corner of the screen. She could probably hit that, considering the position of the phone in her hand. She moved her thumb along the edge of her phone case, then up. *Tap*.

Her phone was set to "vibrate on tap," so she felt the little purr her phone made when she hit the icon. Okay, so theoretically, her text feature was now open. She moved her thumb toward the top of the screen—but not *too* near the top—to where her last text exchange should be. Who had texted her last? Probably Sasha. Sasha was the most patient, the most persistent. She would've kept trying to reach out long after Ray and Liam had given up. *Tap.*

Next she shifted her thumb back down toward the bottom of the screen, where the message box should be. *Tap.* Now the keyboard should be showing. What should she type? She had to say where she was. But her texts were always full of typos even when she could see the keyboard. Trying to input more than a few letters would probably result in total gibberish. And then autocorrect would probably mangle the message even more. *I'm at Neptune Park* could easily turn into *Who's a naughty jerk?*

Well, she'd just have to do her best—and trust that Sasha would know what she meant. *Tap, tap.*

She pictured the location of the SEND key in her mind, hoping the text would go through. A little to the right . . . *Tap.*

15

Sasha

At first, Sasha thought the aftershock had come and gone without changing much.

And then she smelled it: a scent that reminded her of rotten eggs.

Gas.

Crap. We have a gas leak.

That was how most fires started after earthquakes. Gas leaks turned into explosions, swallowing houses in flames.

Instinctively, Sasha reached for her phone— but she'd never manage to get a call through now. Thanks to the aftershock, the cell towers were probably even more jammed than before.

She would have to take care of this herself.

Okay, there's a gas leak. What do you do when there's a gas leak? You shut off the gas.

The gas meter was outside, attached to back of the house. She needed to get to it—fast.

You can do this.

But that had never worked—the *you can* approach. It was too theoretical. It felt too much as if she was trying to trick herself. Like when teachers said, *You can do anything you put your mind to.* Bull. *You can* was what you told people who were failing, people who weren't making progress.

So instead she told herself, *You're doing this.*

That usually worked a lot better.

To shut off the gas valve, she'd need a wrench. Which meant she needed to find her mom's toolkit.

Sasha wheeled herself over to the hall closet. She pulled up alongside the closet door and braced herself. *Everything in the closets has probably shifted*, her mom had said. Taking a deep breath, Sasha pulled open the door.

Her mom's ironing board flew out at her, followed by the iron itself. Sasha managed to use the board as a shield, deflecting the iron, as well as the value pack of tissues that tumbled out of the closet. Everything else seemed to have settled already. Sasha tossed the ironing board to the ground and reached her right hand into the closet, leaning sideways out of her chair to rummage around on the shelves.

The rotten egg smell was getting stronger.

Come on, come on, I know it's in here somewhere . . . She leaned as far to the side as she could, stretching her arm toward the back of the closet.

Aha.

Her fingers brushed the fabric of the tool bag. With her left hand, which still gripped her wheelchair's armrest, she pushed her body up and to the right. Her right hand shot forward just a couple more inches. Now she had a decent grip on the bag. She dragged it forward, over the shelf's remaining clutter—scattered soap bars and spare razors. At last she heaved the bag out of the closet and onto her lap.

The smell of the gas was starting to make her sick to her stomach.

She unzipped the bag and dug around for the wrench. Hammer, screwdriver, pliers, box of drill bits, another screwdriver . . . *If this house explodes just because Mom has too many tools* . . .

Wrench. Got it.

Sasha flung the toolkit onto the floor, gripped the wrench in her right hand, and spun herself into a 180-degree turn. *Move, Hill, move* . . .

The path her mom had cleared through the living room was *sort of* still there. The aftershock had moved the furniture again, but Sasha was able to weave around the obstacles. She shoved open the front door and pushed herself down the slope of cement that had replaced the front steps two years ago.

Wheeling herself on grass always took extra effort. Sasha propelled herself as fast as she could, moving along the side of the house. She pulled up beside the gas meter— the sort-of rectangular gray tank mounted to the siding.

The valve was just a few inches off the ground. She couldn't reach it from her chair. Time to dismount.

She tossed the wrench to the ground and locked her wheels. Then she braced herself against the wall with one arm and gripped the handle of her chair with the other. "Here we go, Peg." Yes, she talked to her wheelchair sometimes. Liam talked to his car—and he didn't even spend sixteen hours a day in it.

Carefully, supporting herself with her arms, she heaved herself out of the chair and eased onto the ground. Now she could get at the gas valve. With the wrench, she cranked the valve's metal notch so that it rotated by 90 degrees.

Done.

Explosion averted.

Getting off the ground was always trickier than getting out of the chair, but she managed it. As her physical therapist liked to say, *Never underestimate a lady's upper-arm strength.* The wrench was still lying in the grass, but someone could come back for it later. Sasha wiped the sweat from her brow. She knew she shouldn't go back inside until the gas company did an inspection, but that could be days from now . . .

Her phone buzzed. A text had come through! Maybe the cell towers were starting to get a handle on the phone traffic.

Sasha expected the text to be from her mom. But it was from Harper.

All it said was *PH*.

A feeling of pure relief punched Sasha in the stomach. She dragged in a deep, grateful breath. If Harper had sent a text, Harper was at least alive.

But—*PH*? What did that mean? Was it just a random pocket-dial, a mistake? Or . . .?

Of course.

She used the video chat app to call Liam again just in case cell service wasn't completely back yet.

Liam's panicked face appeared on her phone screen. "Sasha, you won't believe what just happened—"

"I think I know where Harper is."

"What? Where?"

"Meet me at Neptune Park as soon as you can."

Now she just had to find those mountain bike tires.

16

Ray

"What did she mean, '*Meet me* at Neptune Park'?" Ray demanded as he and Liam cut through an alley. "She's gonna try to get there on her own?"

"You—know Sasha," gasped Liam. He was seriously out of breath, but so far he still managed to keep up with Ray. "There's nothing she—wouldn't try to do."

"Yeah, but doesn't she trust us?"

"I don't think—that's the point." Liam drew a wheezy breath. "I think—she thinks— we should all just—be there."

Ray swallowed. His throat was insanely

dry. He hadn't had a drink of water since lunchtime. "Yeah, I get it. But she did also call 9-1-1, right?"

"Yeah, she said—she'd do that as soon as—we hung up. Obviously if it's—really bad—we'll have to—wait for the pros. But like I said—that's not—really the point—of going over there."

"Yeah," Ray said again. He tried to shake the image of his ruined apartment building, now surrounded by emergency vehicles. Tried not to think about what one of the paramedics had said when Ray approached him a minute ago. *Gotta deal with one thing at a time, kid. Sorry, but we have to stay here as long as we're needed. I'm sure they'll send someone for your friend as soon as they can.*

He tried not to think about the fires that he could smell in the air.

He thought about Harper, his friend, who'd gone back to Neptune Park to look for her lucky keychain one more time. Who'd managed to text Sasha two letters—*PH*.

Prospect Hotel.

The chances that the old building was still standing were slim to none.

Ray tried not to think about that either.

Instead he just thought about Harper, his friend, and how he wasn't done being friends with her.

17

Sasha

Sasha put the 9-1-1 dispatcher on speakerphone and talked as she worked. By the time the call ended, she'd opened all the windows—to get rid of the gas smell—and switched her wheels. Then she shot her message to her mom: *Gas leak, shut off gas, meeting L & R.* No need to freak out her mom with the truth, which would've been more like *Taking unnecessary risks, BRB.* She got the spare key from under the yard edging, locked up, and headed for Neptune Park.

The park was half a mile west of Sasha's house. On an ordinary day, she could get there in ten minutes.

On a day like today, she had no idea how long it would take her. But she was closer than Ray and Liam were right now. And the 9-1-1 dispatcher hadn't given her confidence that a fire truck was rushing to the scene. Edson's emergency response capacity was strained to the limits. Residences and businesses were on fire or partially collapsed with people inside. People right under their noses needed help. Dealing with a girl who *might* be missing and *might* be stuck inside an abandoned hotel was lower on their priority list.

And even if rescue workers were already combing the hotel, Sasha still had to be there. Even if it took her an hour to get there.

The best thing about Peg the Wheelchair was how lightweight it was. And the worst thing about Peg the Wheelchair was . . . how lightweight it was. Big electric-powered chairs were way harder to tip over. But they were also harder to navigate with. Sasha could steer Peg clear of a lot of obstacles. She would have to count on that.

Because the sidewalks and streets were a mess.

Several times, she just had to backtrack when she ran into a major roadblock. A downed power line. A fire truck parked in front of a flaming house. A flooded street, shimmering with water from a burst pipe somewhere.

But other times, she just plowed through or skirted around the problem spots. Her mountain bike tires could safely absorb most of the cracks in the sidewalk, a lot of grit and pebbles—stuff her ordinary tires couldn't handle.

And that tree lying across the sidewalk? Easy enough to bypass. She just had to do a little hop over the sidewalk curb, check that no cars were coming, and continue down the middle of the street. At the corner, where the curb was a gentle slope, she got back on the path.

"Miss, are you all right?" a man called from a second-floor window.

Sasha got this a lot. "I'm fine, thanks!"

In her head, she switched between two thoughts.

You're doing this.

And: *Harper is okay.*

Harper has to be okay.

18

Liam

They saw the hotel from a block away.

Or what was left of it.

"The whole thing fell apart," Liam choked out as he ran alongside Ray. He didn't have much breath to spare.

The hotel was a pile of brick. *Brick*, for goodness sake. Nobody had built with brick in California since, like, 1906.

This is not good, not good, not good.

The last time Liam had felt this painful sense of panic was two years ago, when he'd heard about Sasha's accident. When he'd only known that she'd been rushed to the hospital "in bad shape," which could've meant *dead*.

One look at the rubble of the hotel told Liam what this could mean.

Ray started shouting. "Harper! Harper! We're coming!"

Liam wanted to join in but didn't have enough air in his lungs.

And where was Sasha?

Ray reached the wreckage first. He paced the edge of the brick mountain, still calling Harper's name. Liam caught up just as Ray started climbing.

"Don't!" Liam warned him, heaving in air. "You could—cause a shift. Could crush her. Stay off it."

"Harper!"

"If you—shut up—a second—we might— actually—be able to—hear her."

Ray went quiet. They both listened for Harper's voice but heard nothing.

"Okay," said Liam. He had his wind back now. "It's a big building—*was* a big building. There's a lot of ground to cover. She could be anywhere. Let's circle the whole thing. You go left, I'll go right."

He raised his voice to a shout: "Harper, if you're here and you can't talk, that's okay. But if you can find some way to make noise—if you can tap on something, a piece of metal piping, maybe. Any kind of noise . . . We're listening. We're here. We'll find you."

He started moving along the perimeter of the ruins. Ray headed in the opposite direction. Smoky, bitter air wafted toward them from another part of town. Liam felt his sweat drying in uncomfortable prickles. *Come on, Harper.*

Tap. Tap. Tap.

It was the sound of one dull, hard object against another dull, hard object. Not as clear and piercing as metal-on-metal would've been, but it was audible.

"Here!" shouted Liam. "She's somewhere over here! Good job, Harper! Keep it up!"

Before Liam could stop him, Ray started scrambling over bricks, moving toward the middle of the destroyed structure.

"Be careful, you idiot!" Liam yelled after him—right before he did the same thing.

They stopped about a foot away from the source of the tapping. Ray ripped aside a chunk of the ceiling and stared down through layers of debris. Liam thought he spotted a flash of blonde hair. "Harper?" Ray called. "Tap once if you can hear me."

Tap.

Ray's face split in a huge, stupid grin. "Tap twice if you're glad we're here."

Tap, tap.

"That's freaking emotional blackmail, man," Liam laughed as he wiped the tears from his eyes.

Then he stiffened. "Wait a minute. *Where's Sasha?* She should be here by now."

19

Sasha

"**H**ey, hon, are you okay?"

Sasha was breathing hard, pumping her arms with all her strength, and focusing on the ground in front of her. She knew a vehicle had pulled up alongside her, but she didn't look up when she heard the stranger's voice. Just kept wheeling Peg forward. She was only two blocks from the park. *You're doing this.*

"I'm fine, thanks."

"You sure there's not—someone you'd like to call, or anything?"

"Nope. I'm doing just fine," she retorted, still not looking up.

"It's just—um—is there any way we can help?"

In frustration, Sasha raised her head. The guy talking to her was leaning out of a vehicle that looked like a movers' truck, except that it was bright red. Printed across the side of the trailer were the words *Edson Fire Department, Urban Search and Rescue Task Force.*

Sasha rolled to a stop. "You're not busy?"

"Just had a false alarm on this block. We're between calls."

"In that case," said Sasha, "go straight to Neptune Park. Please. I think my friend is trapped in the Prospect Hotel."

The guy stared at her, completely caught off guard.

"I'm serious!" she snapped. "Go! Right now! I'll meet you there."

"You're sure you'll be—"

She hadn't lost her temper about this kind of thing in a long time, but Harper was worth it. "I CAN TAKE CARE OF MYSELF! WORRY ABOUT *HER!* GO BEFORE I GET ANGRY!"

The truck drove off. Later, when Sasha had time to think about it, she couldn't help but enjoy the expression on the guy's face. He couldn't have looked more astonished if she'd stood up and started walking.

20

Liam

"Thank everybody's gods," Liam sighed. "There's a rescue vehicle."

And his phone was buzzing: an incoming call, through the video chat app, from Sasha.

Liam answered it immediately. Sasha's face appeared, sweaty but otherwise normal. "Are you okay?" he asked. "Where are you?"

"I'm almost there," Sasha panted. "But I sent some help ahead of me. There should be a search and rescue truck heading your way—"

"They just pulled up. I see the dudes getting out now." He glanced at Ray, who was frantically waving to the rescue workers.

"We're flagging them down. And Sasha—we found her. She's here, she's responding to us. That's all we know for sure, but—"

Ray's flailing hand accidentally smacked Liam in the eye. Liam automatically swatted Ray's arm in response.

Sasha saw this but ignored it. She was focused on the important point: Harper was alive. "I'll be *right there*. I'm going to hang up so I can use both hands. Tell her I'm on my way."

Liam grinned. Crap, he was crying again. "I think she knows."

21

Ray

Hospitals were soul-sucking prisons of fluorescent lighting. And yet Ray was glad to be here. Because this was a part of the hospital for people who were going to be okay. At the moment, he'd rather be here than anywhere else.

Harper had two cracked ribs and a dislocated shoulder. Oh, and a "slightly punctured lung," as one of the nurses had called it.

Not that they hadn't all seen worse.

But all three of them showed up ready to pamper Harper.

"Check this out," Liam said to her. "I made a 'We Heart Harper' playlist on my phone. Let's get our dance on up in here." He hit *play* and the faint sounds of eighties techno filtered into the hospital room.

"Feel free to ignore that," said Sasha with a groan. "Here, I made you a card. I had to steal a blank sign-in sheet from the front desk to make it because I didn't have any paper. Oh—I also stole the pen. I should probably give that back on the way out . . . "

"And I," announced Ray, "come bearing seven candy bars. I used up literally all my change at the vending machine downstairs."

It was the best they could do on short notice. Especially considering that only Liam's home was safe right now. Sasha's house still needed the gas issue fixed, and Ray's apartment building was missing its ground floor. Ray and his parents would be staying at Liam's place. Harper's dad, who was currently speaking with a doctor in the hallway, had invited Sasha's family to crash with him for the night.

Harper didn't seem to have a problem with their measly offerings. She was laughing and crying and trying unsuccessfully to sit up in the hospital bed.

"You guys, I'm so sorry for the way I acted before. I can't believe I was so horrible about such a stupid—"

"Harper, it's okay," Ray cut in. "Forget it." Sasha reached out and took Harper's hand.

Harper swallowed a hiccup. "I should've known I could always count on you guys."

"Yeah, you should've," said Liam. "But we really are sorry about Friday. If we hadn't left you behind—if we'd helped you look for your keychain—maybe none of this would've happened."

She shook her head. "It was just a keychain. I mean—it wasn't *just* a keychain, but a lot of things matter more. I shouldn't have gone back for it."

"To be fair, you didn't know an earthquake was about to hit," Ray pointed out.

"Yeah, but that building's been condemned for a long time. I knew it wasn't safe to go poking around in there. I shouldn't have done that, on Friday *or* today."

"I think each of us did at least one stupid thing today," said Ray. "So, we're all in the club."

"Even Sasha?"

"My mom thinks it was pretty stupid of me to go to the park," Sasha said. "She wishes I would've waited for her to drive me—even though driving was also a bad idea. Basically, there weren't many smart options open to me."

"Man, Harper," added Ray, "I wish you could've seen Sasha tearing across the park to get to the hotel. I thought she'd put rocket boosters on Peg."

Harper smiled. "I saw you all when the rescue workers got me out. I'll never forget that."

Liam took one of the candy bars. "Well, to quote our book for English class, all for one and blah-blah-blah, right?"

Sasha laughed. "We're definitely going to fail that presentation."

"On the bright side, school's closed for a while, so we have time to work on it," Liam said cheerfully around a mouthful of chocolate.

Harper laughed too, though she winced a little when it clearly caused her some pain in the rib area. "I'm sure it'll work out fine."

Right then, Ray didn't think about his damaged apartment building. He didn't think about how he and his parents would move on and start fresh together. He didn't think about the days and weeks and months of effort that it would take to rebuild their lives.

He just thought about his friends: Sasha still wearing her mountain bike tires, Liam shamelessly eating a candy bar he hadn't bought, Harper smiling as she looked at each of the others in turn.

They'd been through worse days. They'd get through this one.

DAY OF DISASTER

AFTERSHOCK
BACKFIRE
BLACK BLIZZARD
DEEP FREEZE
VORTEX
WALL OF WATER

Would you survive?

About the Author

Vanessa Acton is a writer and editor based in Minneapolis, Minnesota. She enjoys stalking dead people (also known as historical research), drinking too much tea, and taking long walks during her home state's annual three-week thaw.